*To my parents, Graham and Margaret, for planting the seeds   A.S-B.*
*For Steven, Celeste and Daniel Harrison Gomez with love   E.G.*

Text copyright © 2007 Anna Scott-Brown
Illustrations copyright © 2007 Elena Gomez
This edition copyright © 2007 Lion Hudson

The moral rights of the author and illustrator
have been asserted

A Lion Children's Book
an imprint of
**Lion Hudson plc**
Wilkinson House, Jordan Hill Road,
Oxford OX2 8DR, England
www.lionhudson.com
ISBN 978 0 7459 6049 4 (UK)
ISBN 978 0 8254 6263 4 (USA)

UK first edition 2007
USA first edition 2008
1 3 5 7 9 10 8 6 4 2 0

A catalogue record for this book is available
from the British Library

Distributed by:
UK: Marston Book Services Ltd, PO Box 269, Abingdon,
Oxon OX14 4YN
USA: Trafalgar Square Publishing, 814 N Franklin Street,
Chicago, IL 60610
USA Christian Market: Kregel Publications, PO Box
2607, Grand Rapids, Michigan 49501

Typeset in 20/28 Throhand Regular
Printed and bound in China

# Creation Song

Anna Scott-Brown

*Illustrations by* Elena Gomez

LION
CHILDREN'S

In the beginning there was God.
And not much else.

In fact, apart from God there was
nothing.

So God was all alone.

But God had a plan...

Out in the silent darkness he began to dream.
He dreamed of friendship and laughter,

of little running streams,
and butterfly wings,
of great mountain slopes
and wind in the trees.

Then, from somewhere deep within,
God started to

S  I  N  G.

And his song spread through the formless deep,
running across the void, carrying the longings of God
as far as they could go.

And
when the song stopped,
it picked up the corners of
nothing, folded them neatly
together, and rolled it all up into a ball.
And God held it in the palm of his
hand and saw that it was good.
He breathed on it gently and the
silent sphere drifted into the
emptiness, and stayed
there.

Then with steps as light as the sigh of a moth,
God danced across the surface of nothing.

Everywhere he stepped a tiny prick of light pierced the sleeping shell.
Faster and faster he danced and more and more light broke through.
Something began to stir deep down in the heart of nothing.
It stretched.

A hollow appeared and then a rise.
And instead of nothing there were hills
and there were valleys.

Excitedly all the little points of light
rushed over to see what was happening
and became the

sun.

So God went on
dancing

and created more light –

the stars

and planets.

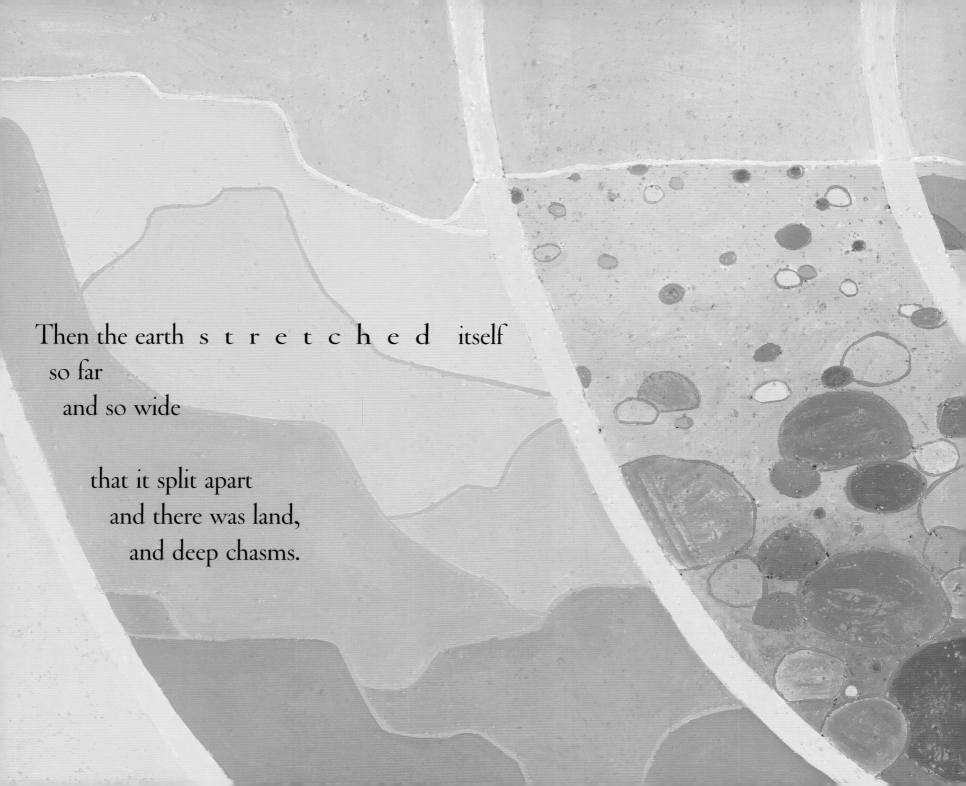

Then the earth s t r e t c h e d itself
so far
and so wide

that it split apart
and there was land,
and deep chasms.

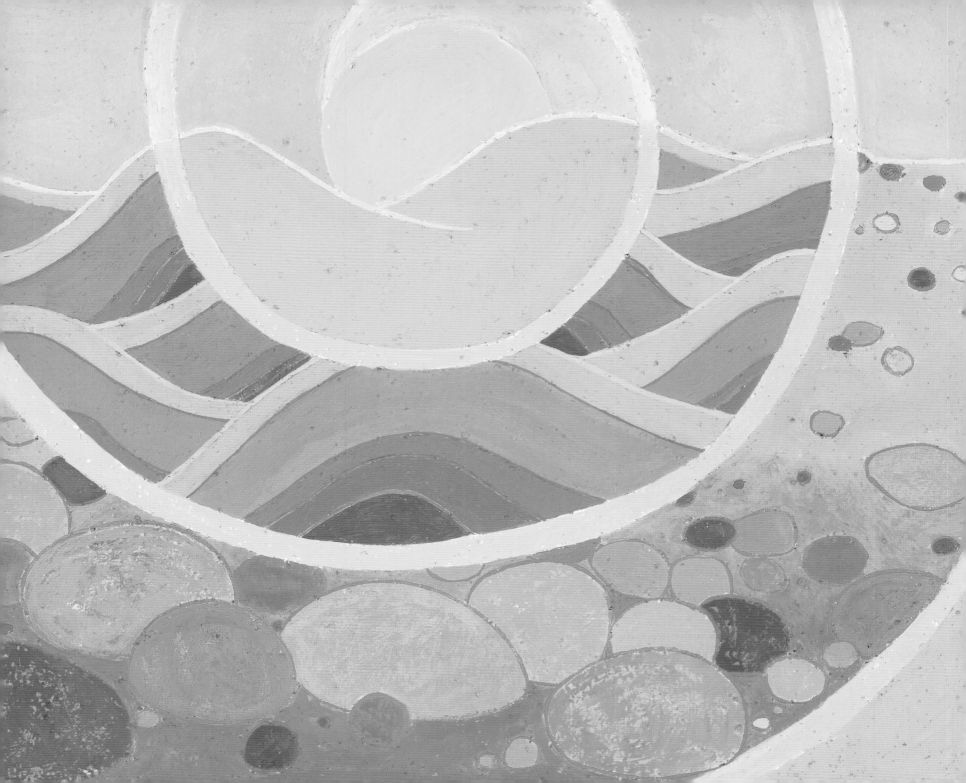

God cried tears of joy and water poured down
through the holes made by the light, and the
seas and lakes and rivers filled up with water.

Eagerly the sun *hurried* over to see –
and reflected in the water there was the moon.

Gladly the small lights danced as God's tears fell
across the earth in rainbow colours.

From the soil beneath, trees
and plants began to grow.

God and Earth began to laugh, and as their
laughter spread the color sped before it,
flowers opened, bushes burst into blossom
and on the trees fruit grew.

On and on the laughter flowed
and where it caught a raindrop
birds flew –
of every shape, and size and hue –

and **filled** the earth
with yet more music.

From on high they landed on the earth, where there were animals of every kind – great herds of zebras, gazelles and towering giraffes.

There were flying lizards, running emus, bleating sheep and calling owls.

And the waters teemed with fish, leaping and swimming in the seas and rivers.

God saw that it was good.
So he stepped down and walked on earth.

Then he began to s i n g once more,
deep deep notes from far within.
Every created thing added its own notes to the music,
which rose and filled the air –
and there was man.

Joyfully God went on singing, higher and higher
and the music wrapped itself around man
and brought forth woman.

Then God began to dance and instead of
nothing there were seals and elephants and
chimpanzees, kangaroos and platypus,
big fish and small fish, flat fish and round fish,
peacocks and hoopees, crested birds and humming birds,

and the wind and the trees, flowers and leaves,
the waters and the waves and all good things,
the sun and the moon and the stars.

And at the centre was God with the two beings he had made in his own likeness. They combined within themselves all the music of his soul and all the love of his heart and all the joy of creation.

All creation
d<small>ance</small>d
with him.